Have You Seen Gordon?

For Olive and Penny.
For everyone who wants to be found and for those who don't.
—A. J. E.

To Rebecca, for finding me in the crowd.
—R. C.

SIMON & SCHUSTER BOOKS FOR YOUNG READERS
An imprint of Simon & Schuster Children's Publishing Division
1230 Avenue of the Americas, New York, New York 10020
Text © 2021 by Adam Jay Epstein
Illustrations © 2021 by Ruth Chan
Book design by Chloë Foglia © 2021 by Simon & Schuster, Inc.
SIMON & SCHUSTER BOOKS FOR YOUNG READERS and related marks
are trademarks of Simon & Schuster, Inc.
For information about special discounts for bulk purchases, please contact
Simon & Schuster Special Sales at 1-866-506-1949 or business@simonandschuster.com.
The Simon & Schuster Speakers Bureau can bring authors to your live event. For more
information or to book an event, contact the Simon & Schuster Speakers Bureau at
1-866-248-3049 or visit our website at www.simonspeakers.com.
The text for this book was set in Garamond.
The illustrations for this book were rendered digitally.
Manufactured in China • 0621 SCP
First Edition
10 9 8 7 6 5 4 3 2 1
CIP data for this book is available from the Library of Congress.
ISBN 978-1-5344-7736-0
ISBN 978-1-5344-7737-7 (eBook)

Have You Seen GORDON?

By Adam Jay Epstein

Illustrated by Ruth Chan

Simon & Schuster Books for Young Readers

NEW YORK   LONDON   TORONTO   SYDNEY   NEW DELHI

PUPSICLES!

Can you find Gordon in the city? Is he eating a hot dog? Is he taking a jog? I bet you can find him.

Can you find Gordon at the farmers market? Is he buying strawberries? Or is he wearing a pink-and-yellow hat that everyone can see very easily? **Gordon!**

What are you doing?

I love this hat!

Well, it makes you really easy to find.

So no hat?

No hat, Gordon. Just hide.

Got it.

O-kay. I suppose we could find someone else to look for.
And change the title of the book.

Sorry to bother you, Jane, but this is important. Don't worry. We only have a few pages left, so it won't take long.

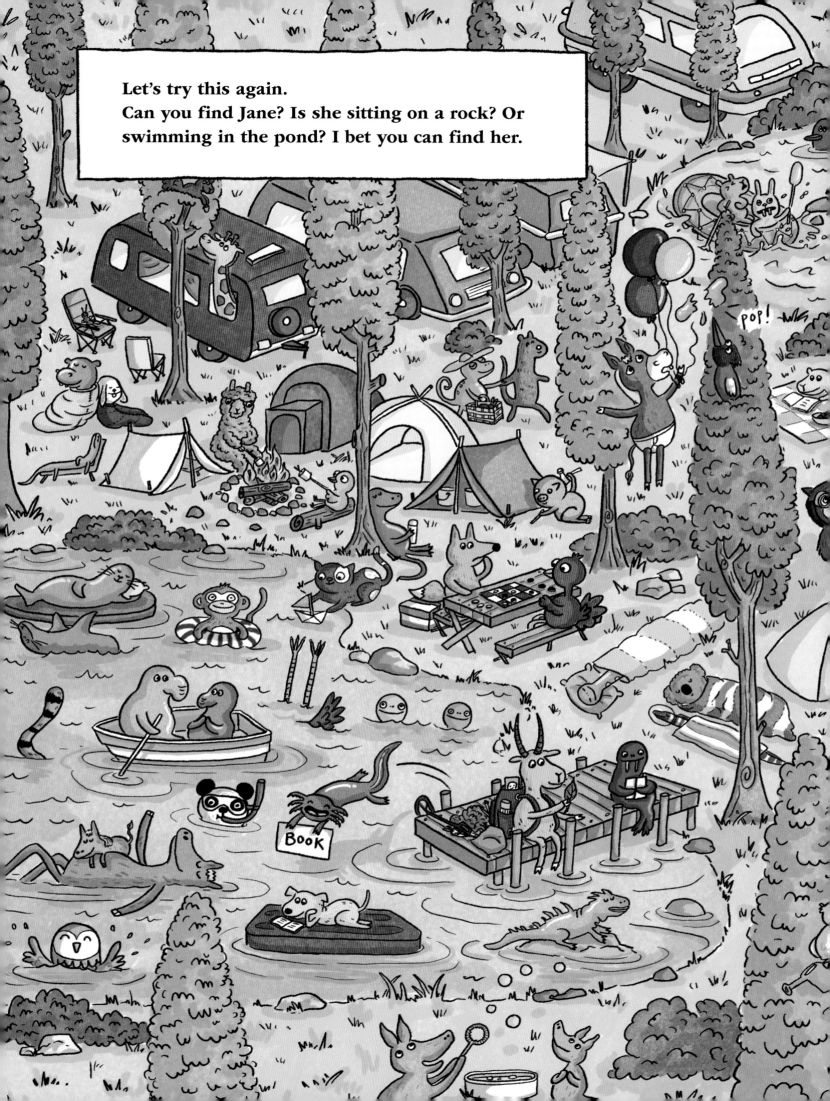

Let's try this again.
Can you find Jane? Is she sitting on a rock? Or swimming in the pond? I bet you can find her.

Can you find a wizard?
The fairy princess?
A scuba diver?

Aren't your eyes getting tired? Mine are.

Can you find the baby with a purple pacifier?
A dragon playing the violin?
A bright copper penny?
A slice of blackberry pie?

It's going to be midnight before you find all of these.

Can you find a couple holding hands?
A jar of pickles?
The space pirate?
A sea monster brushing her teeth?

. . . can you find a pair of friends?